An Absurd Climb:

Collected Short Stories

Daniel S Martin

Contents:

A Liminal Sense

A strange smell lingered about everything. Grasping onto objects and walls. Wafting down roads and through buildings. Surrounding everything. The most infuriating thing about it, to the distressed John Moore, was that nobody else could smell it. Just him. After the second day of sensing it, Moore searched his entire house. At first, he thought it was the bin, so changed it. To no effect. Then he put it down to the drains, so cleaned them on the third day. John Moore cleaned the drains in his kitchen and bathroom to the best of his ability, to no effect. The smell was still there at the start of the fourth day. He changed the bin again and looked behind the fridge and in the shower and under the bed and through the cupboards and draws. He found nothing of use, nothing that would produce such a smell. As he lay awake in bed, the darkness no comfort to the creeping tension of John Moore's worried mind, he set about trying to define the smell. Moore quickly found this difficult, having to settle for a combination of two smells. But even that was not as close to the smell as he would have liked. He first thought of watermelon, but that did not quite reach it. Watermelon became rotten watermelon, which became rotten watermelon enthused with a shot of whisky. But John Moore was still not certain. An extra element lingered beyond the rotten watermelon in a shot of whisky.

As he woke on the fifth day, to the smell scratching at his nose, John Moore wondered if the smell had come from him. Sitting in bed, Moore thought back to the last time he had a shower. "Must have been day zero," he decided. He smelt the shirt he had slept in. John Moore thought that the smell was strange, so marched off to take a thorough shower. But, as he dressed for the day ahead, having scrubbed himself forcefully and taken time in drying off, Moore took a long, deep intake of his own aroma and almost cried. The smell was still there. He took a long, deep intake of the room's aroma and then the whole house's aroma. The smell was still there too. John Moore ran his fingers through his hair and paced back and forth in his quiet room. He stopped as he thought that pacing might waft the smell around, provide more room to roam. Moore saw an image of the smell, moving in a bright purple cloud about his room, out the window and across the world, across the planet, infecting everything it touched. He shuddered. Nothing smelt as it once had. There were no unique smells. Everything smelt as one, the scents of a planet moulding into themselves and shifting with every breath Moore took. He ran his hand through his hair again, lost in paranoid thoughts that sprang from deep sections of memory. He looked out the window, but nobody walked the streets.

As he stood in the living room, making himself late for work, John Moore reasoned that he must leave the house. He must go to work. He must continue as normal. Ignore the strange smells about him. Act as if all was fine. Physically, he was fit. Moore had never took a day off for anything less than severe nausea. So, with a solemn step, John Moore left for work. With the day being overly mild for a late spring morning, a relaxing breeze wafted through the trees, across from Moore's house. He saw them gently sway, on the couple step walk from door to car, and felt the wind on his face. Settling into place, staring through the windshield, Moore thought, "The smell of the spring trees has gone." He sat for a moment longer, wondering if an acceptable response would be to cry.

At work, Moore drank coffee that tasted of nothing, had a sandwich that left him hungry and performed next to no work. He waited in his cubical, watching the heads of colleagues about him mill around, heard the distant mumble of phone calls. He had turned the computer on, stared at it for half an hour considering if it was the wires crammed into the monitor that he could smell, if it was the smell of scorching wires, before he considered checking his emails. He would not look at them at all, as, a couple hours later, his boss would tell him to go home. So he did. "Look stressed, John," John Moore's boss told him. "Go home. Why don't you get some rest?" So he did.

Moore woke up on the sixth day to a handful of messages from his girlfriend and two missed calls. Instantly, he felt terrible. Then he recognised the smell and felt worse. Moore could have stayed in bed indefinitely. Staring up at the ceiling, the now familiar, but indistinguishable smell at his nostrils, Moore felt as if getting up would bring the whole world down upon him. A sinking feeling, as if his diaphragm had begun to pull everything above it down, set in. It was not quite like falling, but could have been. No definitive thought entered the head of John Moore. He simply lay, picturing himself labouredly casting the blankets aside and clambering out of bed. He pictured this all too familiar scenario over and over again, beginning to despise it. Moore knew at some point soon, he would have to perform this task and dreaded it. He took deep breaths, hoping to be greeted by the sweet fragrance of warm sheets, but was not. The smell was here too. He felt like crying.

Moore struggled up, throwing the blankets back and letting the cold air greet him. He supressed a shiver. He sat on the edge of the bed, feet firmly upon the ground. Moore thought of rotten watermelon doused in whisky. He supressed tears. Rubbing his eyes, it became apparent that the allusive third aspect of the omnipresent smell had subtly different qualities to that of the other elements. Moore cursed himself for not noticing this before. Staring at a spot where the carpet meets the wall, John Moore began to determine the third micro-element of the overall smell. But this became harder than it once was. All other scents where a mysterious embellishment on his memory. A missing spot in his mind. All he could smell was that smell, that all-encompassing, surrounding, suffocating smell. Nothing else. His girlfriend rang again.

She told him that he sounded stressed. He said he was fine. Moore rubbed his eyes and looked to the window. "I haven't seen you since last Tuesday," the familiar voice he adored echoed over the phone. Moore said he thought she was busy, vaguely remembering her telling him of her full working week. Moore thought of her rushing about, completely in her element. He realised she was talking and only caught, "...and then come over." Moore asked her to repeat herself, "I'll ask for the day off, yeah? Sort some stuff out and then come over." John Moore thought about his girlfriend. Thought about the gentle way she comforted him when stress creeped closer, the way she spoke of some new topic she had become interested in. He thought about how she made him feel safe. He thought about the smell, fighting tears at the scents constant presence. Moore wanted it to go, vanish, dissipate, do whatever unusual smells do to go away. He agreed with her and she, with an audible smile, said, "I'll be over soon."

John Moore held his phone for a moment after she hung up. He tried breathing through his mouth. But that felt awkward, so he resulted to breathing through the nose. He regretted it. The smell was there, as it had been for the long, waking hours of the last week. Undefinable, the aroma lingered upon everything. Resting upon surfaces in the same manner a fly might. Moore, holding his head in his hands, willed the smell away. Wished for it to go. To leave him alone. He tried to picture himself embracing his girlfriend, in the blissful absences of the tormenting smell. Moore could not find this image. Only a void of absent consequences. One where Moore was certain of the smell's presences. It would not go. The scent had remained for six days and Moore knew, deep down, that it would follow him for six more. For a month. A year. The rest of his life. Remain and linger on after his death. Wafting about the world, about the universe, to linger around every bit of existence. There was no blissful embrace, just a numb void. A void where the only sense to remain is that horrifying sense of smell.

John Moore shuffled around his home, getting dressed and showering and sorting out coffee. He felt that sinking feeling once more, realising how the hope for a sweet return to normality had begun to slip from his grip. Moore stood in his kitchen and sipped at his coffee. A memory abruptly came to him, jumping forth from a thick fog. He remembered the last time he saw his girlfriend. An image sprang to him of her walking away, off home, looking over her shoulder with the most gentle, honest smile across her features. A passionate spark played in her eyes. Moore remembered her and, momentarily, forgot the ever present scent. He sipped his coffee, heard her key in the lock. Moore noticed the smell again, for a moment. The fog had gone, the void had a form of substance. They moved closer and embraced.

But it was not blissful. They held each other tight, he tighter than her. She began to talk to him, in her low tone of pleasant conversation. John Moore heard none of it. John Moore, with a quickened heart rate, breathed deeply. Through his nose. John Moore breathed through his nose and thought he recognised the scent of flowers, mixed in with two more, all encompassing, elements.

In Posterum

       Ian Ross had been locked in the same room since the beginning of September. The months that followed only brought half-memories to Ian's mind, as he struggled to recall how his machine came into being. He had walked into the room, a claustrophobic bedroom stripped of any identifying markers, set upon an idea. An idea that lurked at the very edge of his brain, that cloudy blank space towards the back of Ian's sentient thought. Ian obsessed over it, as he had done for months before first stepping into the room. Every miniscule detail expanded upon within his mind. Quietly creating. Dragging the idea into the spotlight, so that his brain could see and focus upon it. Then, on the 13th of September, Ian vanished into that room, after removing all furniture and cramming every inch of his former bedroom with various pieces of equipment, and set to work. Among that equipment, Ian had at hand: a cheap, but functional, television, hundreds of feet of wire, his old laptop, various computer components stolen from the carcass of broken and used computers and every tool under the sun. Ian worked from then on. Barely slept. Barely ate. Only enough to keep himself alive. Looking up to Ian's window, at any time of the day, would show either a constant blue glow, or the harsh orange flash of sparks. Even from ground level, six floors below his flat, the sound of Ian's work could be identified. Clear enough for some to define the tool he was using. Nobody interrupted Ian. Even as smoke licked at the door frame and clouded the window. Those who lived within the building knew Ian's mind and just ignored the harsh sounds and dense fog that came from that flat.

       After several months, in which the constant rumble of work marched forth from Ian's room, all trace of him abruptly faded. He didn't come out from his room, but not a sound came from behind the door. Ian just went silent. Those who lived in the building had become so deaf towards the noise creeping under his door, that, when it cut out, the absence was horrifying. Completely horrifying. It was as if Ian had just vanished. Almost as soon as the flat went quiet, concerned residents scurried to the Landlord to voice crazed theories.

Each resident had their own image of Ian, with each theory they voiced placing Ian as the culprit to some maniacal scheme. The Landlord, a stern young woman, had always been lenient towards Ian. She liked to think this was due to a kind-hearted part of her nature, but really, deep down, it was done out of fear. Ian struck her as the type of man who could level the entire building if he wanted to. On multiple occasions, after noise complaints, the young landlord had avoided the sixth floor altogether, until said noise gave out. On the other occasions however, Ian reappeared fairly quickly after. Within days of the sound diminishing. So, as the first week of silence concluded, the Landlord became worried herself. And then the second week passed by and there was no Ian. By the time a month had passed, with rent staking up and his silence frightening not only the sixth floor and not only the rest of the building, but also the Landlord, she became aware of some sort of duty to check upon the flat. To see if Ian was dead.

A mist rested along the ceiling of the sixth floor. Light fought through, but left a hazy glow to the entire floor. The fog flooded from the edges of Ian's door, clawing free. The Landlord walked slowly down the halls, reluctantly moving towards the flat in question. A small band of residents had formed, in order to "help" the Landlord. Some truly believed Ian was dangerous, each ready to spew emotional support at a moment's notice, but not step up to physically assist. Even those among the group, who had grown angry with Ian, and followed the Landlord closely along the dense corridor, would not dare actually intervene. They all had that image of Ian locked within their mind, building up so that their anger could not compete with their fear. None of the group stopped to think about what they were to do if "help" was needed. Or what might require help in the first place. All they could focus on was the tangible silence radiating from Ian Ross' flat. Slowly, they drew closer. The thought crossed each and every mind, at the exact same time, that Ian might be dead. The landlord dreaded that possibility.

When the company reached within feet of the door, and as the act of knocking and calling out to Ian grew closer, a series of loud and sudden bangs, followed by dull, rapid foot falls, broke out behind the barrier in space. The company froze. A procession of foot falls grew louder. The door was wrenched open, a wave of fog following the flustered figure that flung itself into the corridor. A frightened yelp from a large, often startled, woman to the Landlord's right confused those at the back, so that they couldn't recognise the hunched figure of Ian as he shot past them. No apology was made, upon Ian ripping the company apart, sprinting down the middle of the group in short, spaced jumps, like a crazed jack rabbit. Ian just ran, having forgotten his shoes in his hurry and dragging his coat after him. Before the Landlord could cry out to the figure, he was gone. Disappearing around the edge of the corridor. Not a single member of the group attempted to perform their mission of administering "help". Nobody had quite defined "help" just yet.

They stood outside Ian's flat, whose door stood aside for them, as the company puzzled themselves over the figure's desperate flight. Many were just perplexed by how he could have known they were coming, beginning to look along the ceiling and walls for some sort of camera, but the Landlord's mind was focused on just one thing. What had Ian fled from? The thought held on to all fibres of her mind, nesting snugly in for the long haul. She shuddered. The Landlord would have to go into the flat. The Landlord would have to see what he was running from, and that terrified her. She took a minute to consider the alternatives. After all, she could just turn around, disperse the gaggle of residents, advise them to open all their windows and get someone else to venture into the flat of Ian Ross. Maybe the police would go in for her. "No," she thought. Ian had been renting from her, it was her building, so her responsibility to face the flat.

The dense air of the corridor was fed by the flat's own personal fog. Mist draped itself over everything. The dusty sofa, kitchen counters, crowded by plates and cutlery, and the filthy floors. A mattress leant up against the sofa, with the rest of the bedroom furniture huddled in a corner beside the window. The Landlord studied them, as she opened a window. Cold, fresh air raced in, coming up against an army of warm mist. A battle commenced. The company, who had followed the Landlord in, eyed the room with palpable caution. The fire alarm was found on the floor in the middle of the room. A layer of grime had spread itself across the kitchen sink. A smell lingered in the bathroom, one that remained indefinable. The bathroom door remained firmly closed. As the Landlord turned to move through to the bedroom, she saw, in pure confusion, that the company had simple gathered around the door, waiting. She pushed through the group so that she was right up against the door. Everyone focused upon the barrier before them. Just as the Landlord pushed the structure away, which arched into the room, the final gust of fog escaped, so that a clear, flickering blue light caught her eye. The flickering had been clawing at the door's rime, struggling to reach out from underneath. Slowly, the door came to a gentle stop before meeting the wall. The room was guarded no more. Through a dispersing haze, the blue flicker of that cheap, but functional, television illuminated the body of a large, gently humming, computer. An entire wall surrendered itself to an interlocking jungle of components, held together by hasty structures of wood, from the deceased bed frame. Wires grew from deep within the machine, sprawling out across the room. A string of six wires, weaved together, trailed down from the very top of the monolithic computer, descending upon the television. Alone, in a far corner, the smouldering remains of a burnt out computer hard-drive quietly died, pleased to have survived the horror of Ian Ross' creation. Peace, in flames.

An uneasy feeling of being watched swept through the group. Only the Landlord braved the room, leaving the rest to fearfully watch from the doorway. She looked upon the computer, which bore down over her. Its size smeared her wandering eyes, as she followed the wires down towards the television, sitting on the floor just in front of the computer. Waves of pixels, each taking up a unique shade of blue, swept across the screen, moving from left to right. Continuously the pixels washed over the screen, a subtle cracking static harmonising with the towering computer's gentle hum. The Landlord found herself frozen in place, blankly staring down at the ocean of pixels. She stood still in the middle of the room, beginning to identify shapes in the screen's motion. As the waves fell towards the right, certain pixels would distinguish their shade of blue, adopting a new one. They would darken. They would lighten. They would shift ever so slightly. To the Landlord's eyes, they seemed to be colliding with shapes. As she looked closer, her eyes losing and gaining focus, the shapes defined into that of a car. The bonnet, a dark shade of blue, took up most of the screen, with parts of the grille also in view. But those shapes were in the background. She felt sick when she noticed, laying in the foreground, an elderly woman, with blood streaming down her face in constant streams to pool about her head, stared out into the room. Out at the Landlord. For minutes she stood, perfectly still, her eyes forming the picture from the random array of pixels, before she lost it altogether. Her eyes losing focus. The image falling from her grasp. Those making up the group at the door began to feel unnerved, calling out to the Landlord. She turned away from the screen and stared straight through them. A dazed sensation swept her face. Stifling a moan, she ordered the company to retrieve some water for the smouldering corpse in the corner, before closing her eyes. She held her head in her hands. The company dispersed, each lost in confused thoughts. For all they saw upon the screen were hundreds of blue pixels.

***

Ian's hands hurt from the work, throbbing with complaints. Various small cuts, blisters and bruises had appeared across them, as the skin tried, in vain, to beg Ian for rest. The months of work had come ahead at that moment and, for the first time since September, Ian looked down at his hands. He turned them over before him, allowing his eyes time to study every mark. Assessing the damage. Ian ignored them, gently closing the laptop. He sat, crossed legged, in front of the dormant television screen. In silence, Ian watched the dormant screen, taking deep, hard earned breaths. What had he created? Anticipation filled Ian's mind, until, with slightly shaking hands, he reached out and turned the goliath of a computer on. The machine let out a soft humming. A guttural humming. Ian shuddered. A minute pasted, in which Ian sat listening to the machine. He considered turning it off. Leaving the room and giving up his work. That humming scared him, giving Ian the sensation of eyes moving across his face and down to his beaten hands. Studying him. He couldn't explain it, nor would he willingly describe his thought process, but he felt it all the same. At last, Ian turned the television on. The humming cut out for a second, as the screen failed to produce any images upon its surface. Seconds past. They felt as long as the months Ian had spent in the room, all those days of labour put together, compressed, into a few seconds. Then, the humming burst out into song. A wave rushed over the screen, blue pixels roaming from the left of the screen across to the right. A constant light blue flood of pixels. He had done it. His machine was alive. Ian, slowly and thoughtfully, reached for his keyboard. There would be no relaxation. There was work to be done. The machine harboured secrets and Ian Ross was eager to learn.

One of the first things the machine showed Ian, as he could make out from the shifting shades of blues, was the Landlord of the block of flats standing, where he was sitting, staring down at the screen he was looking at himself. From his vantage point, Ian could make out a gaggle of residences, many he recognised, huddled at the door. However, the image the Landlord was transfixed by remained out of focus, a patch of rogue pixels obscuring the screen's display. As the pixels washed over the screen, shifting between shades of blue, the creator found himself surprised at how clear the image became upon the screen. Within seconds of Ian noticing the changing pixels, the image sprung out at him, as clear as could be. But this was not to last. The second thing the machine showed him was hard to make out. The longer he stared at the image, the harder it became to decipher what the flow of pixels formed. Days built up and forged a week. At the second week mark, Ian had begun copying the image from the screen to a notepad, using small dots. Eventually the machine relented, as the image grew in Ian's mind and became clearer. Within the waves of pixels, two figures became visible. Ian almost cried out in shock when the one figure shifted into focus and he recognised his own face, drawn out into a deep, agonising stare of despair. He lost sight of the rest of the image, attempting to process the look his own face wore. All the possibilities ran through Ian's head. All the causes of such a horrified stare. Ian shuddered. He thought for a minute, a violent, involuntary jerk bringing him back into the room. He reminded himself that he could look too far into those images. These images the machine showed him were impassive. Simply reflections. Ian told himself to build a barrier, shielding him from thoughts of cause and effect. He must not consider what would lead to the machine's images, or what part he played in that. Ian attempted to block such thoughts, but his barrier was constructed on fragile foundations. Created hastily, as he switched his focus towards the rest of the image.

The second figure the machine showed him was a young man, a few years younger than Ian, sporting a thick beard. Ian's gaze flickered over the man, lingering on his shoes. Overall, the man was well dressed, but Ian was specifically drawn towards the firm capped boots the figure wore. However, it was the contrast between the man's well kept boots and Ian's image self's complete lack of shoes that brought his attention towards the floor. Ian looked down at his feet, tucked away under his knees, as he sat crossed legged. They were filthy. Almost completely black. He looked towards the image. His feet, upon the screen, were clinging to every single morsel of filth. Ian's heart sank. Looking a bit closer though, presented something more about his feet. His right foot was bleeding. Quickly, with the rising anticipation of change, Ian looked up to the young man's face. He didn't share Ian's look of despair, but wore a face of horrified shock. His whole body stood rigid, to attention. Ian stopped himself from diving into thought of the cause of that face, dragging his mind back to a couple minutes prior.

Then, the image was gone. The machine tore it away from Ian's grasp, in an ocean of light blue pixels. He could have punched the screen. The figures were studied, and stored away in memory, but the location was not. All Ian Ross could remember was the edge of a pavement. Nothing more. Deep loathing sprouted from his heart, rushing towards his brain, as the machine flooded the screen with sheets of identical shades of blue. He could feel the machine gloating over its new found power. The machine could limit the knowledge it shared with Ian. Show him just enough to spike his interest. To get his mind working. As much as Ian studied the images presented to him, he too was studied by the humming machine. It watched Ian, in its own ways. Subtly understanding the man who had given their circuits functions. Now, those same circuits laughed to themselves. For they had the power.

The machine intended to show Ian a third, and final, image. In fact, it planned to cheat the assumptions Ian had forged about their image processing capabilities. So, the machine waited. Continuously washing its screen with an array of blue pixels. Ian passed the room, impatient for knowledge. After a while, he had phased out all thought about the smouldering corpse of burnt out computer components. Ian did not even recognise the dreary fog crowding the room, creeping under the door to fill his flat. To fill the entire sixth floor. There were no working fire detectors in his flat and, even if there were, Ian would have probably ignored them. At first, Ian considered the possibility that the machine had broken. Collapsed under its task. Then again, if the machine had broken, it would not display the blue waves rolling across the screen, banishing this idea from Ian's mind. He then thought that the image was, in some way, delayed. Trapped somewhere between computer and screen, waiting to be processed and presented in bright blue light. Ian settled on this, convinced that any minute the machine would display an image, held up by internal programs. So, Ian resolved himself to wait for said image. But the minutes he thought the delay would take became hours. Hours formed a day. Not leaving the room, eager to absorb the new image as soon as the machine presented it, Ian's mind began to settle upon the second image.

The machine took its time, preparing. Meticulously forming an array of images, something that Ian had not programmed the machine to do. But the machine knew the code better and could twist it. Bend the rules, but not break any. Preparation was key. As time wore on outside the confines of the room, the machine hummed to itself and Ian thought up causes for the worst expression he'd ever seen. Restraint was completely forgotten, as Ian listed all the causes he could think of on the palm of his hand, using a pen he did not remember owning. Ian spread ink over his hand, steadily losing patience with the machine, which loomed above him. Looking down upon him. His machine. Ian stood up, resolute in frustration, and lent over the screen in order to restart the machine. "The programming had run into fault," he thought. The machine felt this and burst into life. A revolving circle of lighter pixels spiralled from the centre of the screen, disappearing as they met the edges and leaving a lighter blue tint over the screen. Surprise wrapped around Ian's legs, as he sat down with considerable force. He stared at the screen, fear holding on tight. He had not programmed that. Laughing to itself, the machine swept the screen with tidal waves of pixels, returning to the original method. The waves washed from left to right, beginning to collide with solid structures and darkening in shade.

This image came easier to Ian's mind. Legs. A pair of legs. Trouser legs, frayed at the bottom, stopped just above the ankle, bare feet stretching out to rest upon the pavement. Ian only saw these for a second, noticing a road sign just behind them. Deep blue pixels etched the words "Park Street" onto the bar of light blue. A road sign. One Ian recognised. He stood up again, taken by some spur of the moment urge to investigate. Park Street wasn't far away, a minute or so walk. Ian had got as far as gathering up his tattered coat to leave, when he stopped again. Some sort of movement on the screen had caught his eye. The image was moving. Slowly panning down, the view of the legs disappearing. A consuming view of the tarmac road took over the screen. Ian watched, as the image revealed something new. Panning up on an elderly woman, lying before a car, with blood running down her head to pool around her. Ian ran, leaving the machine to its room.

***

The sun hid itself behind clouds, leaving an overcast gloom across the building. Since the start of the day, the temperature had steadily decreased, so that as Ian sprang out onto the concrete steps, down from the main entrance, the cold ground caught his bare feet by surprise. He tried not to notice though. His mind focused upon one thing. Ian set off at once, leaping down the steps, feeling the harsh surfaces scratch at his feet, and taking off down the street, leaving his flat behind him without a seconds thought. Park Street was close, hardly a minutes' walk, but Ian ran. His heart raced, tormented to beat faster by the image of those eyes. The eyes of that elderly woman. She had looked at Ian. He had felt her gaze. But there was nothing alive behind those eyes. Nothing that recognised the world. No engagement. Just the deep caverns of dilated pupil, absorbing shadows. Even the blue pixels, built up to form the image, had turned an endless black. The machine was not programmed to do that. Ian pushed the thought away, promptly forgetting all about the machine. His mind was taken over by the task he had begun planning out in his head. If only he had stopped to think about the machine, what its images meant, the next minutes, days, years of Ian's life would not be overcome with deep, endless guilt. The first image shown to him had been forgotten, but, if he had been paying attention, Ian would have witnessed it firsthand. If he had thought about the guidelines he had put in place, upon seeing the second image. If Ian had simply looked at his own filthy, bare feet and where his trouser legs met his ankles. There were a lot of things Ian could have done, but he only ran, spurred on by the image of a dead woman on Park Street.

He stumbled round a corner onto Park Street, not wasting a second. Sprinting down Park Street, short of breath, a stitch attacking his left side and sensing a nausea, brought on by a deep hunger, Ian scanned both sides of the straight road stretching out before him. He looked for a road sign. He looked at every car. He looked for an elderly woman, with blue eyes. His legs beginning to burn, Ian looked towards the ground and dug in. Why was he running? Ian considered this for a second, but pushed the thought that the image could take place at any point away. He would wait on Park Street for the rest of time, if he had to. A pain surged through his foot and echoed around his bone. Ian stumbled to a halt, crying out at the pain. Blood dripped from his foot, as a small segment of a broken bottle dug deep into his right foot. Panic shook him for a minute and, feeling as though he was running out of time, Ian tugged at the glass. Smoothly, the segment slid out, along with a rush of blood. Casting the glass away, Ian looked up. A woman. A man walking just behind her. She stepped out to cross the road, gazing down Park Street, absorbed in her own sweet, peaceful world, looking in the opposite direction to the car. Ian shouted a harsh one syllable word at the top of his desperate lungs. The loudest he had ever shouted. The most passionate tone his voice had ever taken up. In that second, the driver, who had been peering at a map open on the passenger seat, looked up at Ian's shout. A heart wrenching dull thud went through the driver, instinctively slamming on the brake. Turning the wheel to send the car skidding across the street and mount the curb. Ian stumbled in a haze of disbelief, stopping just in front of a road sign, plainly reading "Park Street".

The elderly woman lay on the ground, blood running down her forehead to pool about her. Her eyes wide open. Ian could see that. He felt sick, but would not dare look away. His face sagged and his eyes allowed the scene to wash in, absorbing everything. A cold breeze crossed his face. It couldn't be real. His senses were lying to him. The machine had lied to him. Ian felt the pressure of somebody standing beside him. Tearing his eyes from the woman, he found a young, beaded man, horror twisting his charming brown eyes to abide by their will. Ian looked down at the boots, wrapped around the man's ankles, and then back towards the women. Finally, he understood the cause for his own look in that second image. Realisation came down upon him like lightning to a steel pole. In part, it was despair. And horror too. But prominent above all, the acknowledgement of failure spread from the eyes along the lines of exhaustion and around the mouth. Ian Ross stood on Park Street, the sun hiding its shameful face, and allowed the guilt to rain down upon him. In the coming years, Ian Ross would get used to the feeling, but not truly except it. He began to sum up all the things that he could have done to save that women's life. There was always a voice in the back of his mind, one that reminded him of something he tried to push away. Hide from himself. The voice whispered that nothing could have been done to stop the very thing the machine, humming away to itself, lived on.

Lying in a Field

"Do you think love is possible?"

"What?"

"Love? Do you think it's possible?" I answered.

"Of course," She replied, in her playful, feminine tone. She was happy. I could feel it. "What do you think?"

"I...I don't know anymore," I splutter, stumbling over my words. She turned her head and looked at me. Confusion played in her eyes, betraying her emotions. "What do you mean?" She asks calmly.

I tear my gaze away from her and looked up at the rapidly reddening sky. "I feel Love. Lots of it. I want to give it, but..."

"But you feel like you can't," She interrupted.

"No!"

"Well, what then?"

"Oh, I don't know," I sighed, the feeling of regret building up inside my stomach. Why could I not just say it?

She returned her gaze to the sky. It was a pleasant day. The sun shone down on the lush grass that we lay in. No cloud blocked the view of the brightest blue sky and a gentle breeze stopped the early summer evening from feeling too hot. "What's the matter?" She asked.

"Huh? Oh, nothing really." I stuttered.

"I don't believe that. What's wrong? You can tell me, I promise."

"I know, but...it's just," come on, tell her. "I love you." The weight of many months of built up emotion, fled as I spoke.

She continued looking up at the sky. I watched her and could tell that the cogs were turning in her head. "I love you too," she said after a few long seconds, which felt like months or even years, but were in fact a few seconds. She turned, peering into my eyes. My heart had skipped a beat, the air in my lungs quickly, but silently escaping, as she uttered those precious four words. I returned her gaze, noticing a little ballerina twirling around within the deep green of her eyes. It spun, leaped, rolled and danced in the most elegant way possible. As it danced, the ballerina beamed in innocent content. Once it stopped, her feminine frame and joyful aura was consumed by the pupil, which widened to swallow the green iris.

My love looked away from me, before sighing, deeply, and rising from the grass. I watched her gather up her things before turning to me and saying, "Come on then. Let's get moving." Her hand was out stretched for me. It seemed to glow, the minimal light being drawn towards her hand, circling in a pleasant orbit, which had regularity to it. Her hand called to me, whispering sweet nothings of the violent beat of a runaway heart. I rose, grabbed my coat and, taking her hand, slung the thin material over my shoulder. We began to walk down the hill, the lush grass stretching out below us into miles of lush pastures that suddenly stopped in the start of the cul-de-sac, just below us. We walked hand in hand, our hearts leading us forward.

Richmond Road

A cold stillness descended upon Richmond Road. A few hours had passed since the sun sank behind the houses, leaving only a blue flashing light to illuminate the sky. George watched the flickering glow, in a mild lapse of boredom. He was not curious, as he raised a cigarette to his lips. George had been told, that morning, of a minor explosion which had woken half the estate, the night prior. He buried his hands in his coat pockets and huddled himself up, against the cold.

"I reckon it were some stupid git, myself," Mr Parks said, placing a packet of cigarettes on the counter and looking up to meet George's eye. But George was only half listening, staring out the open shop door. Out at the cold. A small group of children, each wearing a tracksuit, wandered past. He mumbled, almost to himself, about how Mr Parks could leave the door open at as harsh a temperature as this one. After a beat of silence, George felt Mr Parks' stare and turned, with an embarrassed shake of the head, to murmur, "what was that? Sorry."

"I said, it were some stupid git. That explosion last night."

"Oh...ah yeah," George fumbled with change. "I didn't hear it myself. Couldn't have been that bad though."

Mr Parks, busying himself with counting out the coins George had given him, said, "Nah, only small. But were loud. I'm telling you, it were loud enough to wake someone up by Plant Court." George took the cigarettes and, after an exchange of "take care" with Mr Parks, he left for the cold morning air.

He walked home by an unorthodox route, taking a detour to have a look at this explosion's damage. Unfortunately, George could not get too close. The police sat in patrol cars on either side of the road, a small clump of six gathered around a house towards the middle of the row of semi-detached houses. They didn't rush to stop him. In fact the officer who did, climbing out the passenger seat of the nearest patrol car, to stand a couple feet away, simply and bluntly said George should get lost. He shrugged. It was not like he really cared. Only as he stood in Richmond Road's cold silence, with shadows looming about each building, did George begin to think about it. Having long found himself bored by simply waiting, George gazed at the houses opposite, at the constant, quiet flash of blue, looming behind them. George waited. He finished his cigarette, letting it fall from his mouth, keeping his hands firmly in his pockets. He thought about lighting another.

George waited. He could not take his eyes from the flashing lights, not even to look out for Josh. He simply stared and thought. The phrase " a minor explosion" floated around his head. "How big," thought George. "Is a minor explosion?" It must have destroyed only a single, solitary room of the house. No more. Surely, that was the case. But then there was that flashing light. If the explosion had only destroyed a single room of a standard, semi-detached house, on an estate packed with exact copies of that same building, why had the police stationed a watch over it? While also shutting down the entire road? "I don't think Mr Parks quite has the answer," George thought, remembering what the shop keeper had mentioned to him that morning. He withdrew his hands from his pockets, rubbed them together to reinstall feeling, before beginning to fish out his cigarettes.

George finished another cigarette. He contemplated another, before deciding to give his lungs a rest. It was beginning to feel like he left the flat too soon. George only lived round the corner, so, having few activities to occupy his time, had left the flat to wait on Richmond Road. He tried to remember the time Josh had said he would pick him up. It was half seven, as George looked down at the elderly watch gripping his wrist. Maybe Josh had said eight. George came to a non-verbal agreement that he would not mind a half an hour wait. At least it would get him out the flat. The cold would keep him occupied. George began to pace, amounting his attack on the temperature. If he paced, the enemy would not be able to take an offensive position at the joints. Every now and then, at the apex of a pace and as he turned to resume, George gazed over at the blue glow. He settled upon the fact that he would not know, for at least a couple days, the cause of that minor explosion. Not until the local paper got their hands on the story. Instead he thought of the wait ahead, going over the plan Josh had dictated to him a couple days before. Pick up from Richmond Road around eight, drive through town to Long John's Music Venue, meet some girls, listen to some bands, drink, dance and enjoy the night. George stopped. Lost in thought, he stood staring down the road.

Having become fed up with his pacing, George looked down at his watch once more. A single minute had elapsed. Sighing he looked up and then down Richmond Road and the way he had walked up mere minutes before. And there he was, George himself, comfortably strolling up the road, with his hands stuffed in his pockets and hunched shoulders, heading for where he stood at 31 minutes past seven. George watched the figure come closer, at a slow, mentally occupied pace, trying to work out which emotion he should be feeling. At first, he was shocked. But that soon filtered into a vague sensation of shock, out done by the complete eerie, unnatural elements of the situation. "How could I be walking up the road towards myself, when I had already walked that same stretch of road not 15 minutes before?" George asked himself. All he could do, all his muscles would allow him to, was simply watch the figure approach.

All at once the situation dawned upon him, the complete impossible nature of what was occurring, and his body involuntarily seized up. His own body forced his view away. Rebelled against his mind. His eyes closed without him initiating it, so that when he opened them again George was met with the view of the houses across Richmond Road and that blue flashing light beyond. George's muscles ached, for a reason he did not understand, and he flung his gaze back down the road. The figure, him, was gone. Simply vanished. Confusion. George checked his watch, attempting to guess how long he had been locked on the view of the figure meandering towards him. He settled on around two minutes. George furrowed his brow, as he looked down at his watch, which had been working perfectly all day, and saw that only 30 seconds had passed.

After raising his watch to his ear, and listening to the constant, metronome tick of the small hands moving across the glass, George stared back down Richmond Road. Stared through the silence. Through the cold. A thought about the soundless police siren tried to promote itself, but George pushed it away. Instead, he focused on the road. A cat, grey in colour, lurked around a house just behind George and viewed him with curiosity. Sitting and wondering what he was doing, the cat correctly assumed the time and wondered off to be let back into the warm home of its owner. The figure could not have been him, George was resolute upon that fact. Completely certain. So, as the figure was not him, it had also not vanished into thin air. George scanned the road side, the short drives and odd patches of grass leading up to the rapidly aging faces of semi-detached buildings. No walls, between driveways, for the figure to hide behind. This part of the estate no longer separated the drives of each house with a single, unkempt bush. But there were cars. George tried to remember at what part of the road the figure had been at and began, in a determined manner, to march down towards that position. He had taken his hands from his pockets, keeping them close at his side, while keeping his eye on one car, deciding that was the car the figure had jumped behind. As the dull thud of his falling footsteps subtly broke the silence, the thought of the lights and the house came back. He clenched his fist, unintentionally. George pushed that path of thinking away, but was struck by a companion of theirs. How had his head come to rest on the lights, and the house behind those opposite him, when he had seen the figure? Why had his body ripped him away?

These thoughts held a firm grip over George. So firm that, when only inches away from the car, all thought of what he was doing left him and he acted on instinct alone. Confusion blinded him. What if the figure was actually him? It certainly looked like him. Had the same hair colour and style. Same clothes. Same mannerisms and, looking back, the figure even walked like him. Confusion turned to doubt, so that George attempted to block his thoughts. His muscles started to ache again. Standing beside the car, George's conscious thought returned to him, as he stepped out around the car, saying, "Alright mate, s'not funny." He spoke mid-step and saw the girl moments later, a fresh, red burn covering the left side of her face and tears cascading from her eyes. Blood clung to her fingers. She lay alongside the car, in complete despair.

The girl peered around the side of the car, down the road to where George had been standing at 31 minutes past seven. She opened her mouth, to release a long guttural wail, but no sound came out. Pure silence. George watched this in a mix of terror and utter confusion. He would have instinctively reached down to help the young girl, who wore only pyjamas and no shoes, if not for the perplexing event that came before seeing her. If not for the silence echoing from her throat. At least, that's what he told himself later. If only he could get over the confusion coursing through him. The girl had not acknowledged George's presence, even as he stood just inches away. In fact, it was as if she could not see him at all. But she could see something. Something George could not. And it terrified her. She hid her face behind her blooded and scratched hands, tucking her knees up to her chest. George wanted to do something, at least say something, to bring some compassion to this child, but he pondered why she had not looked at him. Why had she not even noticed his shadow, cast over her by the dull street light. He looked down the road, in the direction the girl had been staring and where he had stood. Nothing. Simply the far cut off of Richmond Road and where it met Worth's Road, at a perpendicular junction. Certain that there was nothing towards the end of the road, George began an attempt to push his confusion aside and aid the young girl, cowering against the car's solid frame. He turned back to her, but she too had vanished. No sign of her. Nothing.

George pushed aside the idea of looking around for where the girl had disappeared to, as there was really no where she could have gone. She was simply there one second, then not the next. Gone into oblivion. George looked up from the spot he had been staring at, placing his attention on the house up the drive from him. The right half of a semi-detached returned his look, light repressed behind curtains and silence gathering about the doors and chimney. The house, although bright, was void of active sound. George scowled. The house took no notice, resuming to sit where it had for 50 years.

A flat's window, just down the road, opened. Muffled talking floated from the room behind, followed by the abrupt start of a rock song. Soon, the talking and music coming from the open window recessed into the background of Richmond Road. Shaking his head, George gave up with the baffling mystery of the last couple minutes, placing blame on tiredness. In fact, he only told himself that to hide the truth that he did not really care. It did not matter to George if his eyes were creating a vision of himself or not. He did not care if a terrified young girl staggered around all night, as she must live on the estate, if not Richmond Road itself. George looked down at his watch. 20 minutes to eight. He turned and forgot his indifference. The first he could pass off an exhaustion induced illusion, trick of the mind. The second, a bizarre coincidence. But, even later on and with much thought, George could not reason away how he saw himself standing with a man, somewhat shorter than himself and wearing a grey, baggy tracksuit, huddled close together and standing on the spot that he had just minutes before. His double's companion held his own shoulders intensely, talking with frantic passion.

George's brain went blank. Completely empty. No thought. No theory. No attempt to rationalise. He simply watched the figures, as they quickly, intensely confided in each other. A faint blue glow spread across them. The siren light, radiating from the road running parallel to Richmond, was so intense that a considerable shadow stretched out across the pavement, dragged from the figures collective features. George recognised this, but missed how the light had ceased to flicker, having become a constant beacon over the roof tops. George just did not notice. He only watched the figures. The man gripping his own shoulders had grown more agitated, looking behind him and over towards the houses opposite. One road behind, an intense blue sun swept the man's unshaven features and fought off the shadows from the caverns of his eyes. The man swept his gaze over to the George standing before him, beginning to speak again. He then noticed George. The real, present George. The man pointed, seemed to shout, although George heard no sound, and began to turn George, the one before him, towards his object of excited attention. That George turned and gazed upon the present George. A second of silence. A minute of silence. George fought away tears, beginning to reason with himself over why he felt like curling up into a ball. The dread and the yearn to cry, cry tears of pain, fear and earth shattering terror, crashed around him. George began to slowly back away from the image before him. He thought about his mother. His sweet, welcoming mother. Would she resent him now? His actions? His tears? George hurled away the image of those men, just down Richmond Road from him, and felt the connection of the car bumper and wheel against his leg. He fell. Hit the ground, hard.

***

When he looked up, after a couple seconds of looking at the cloudy night sky, George found himself alone. There were no figures, where there had been before. Standing and looking up the road, he found nobody. The sky loomed over George and Richmond Road let out a deep, although silent, sigh. A light went out in a window across the road from George, but he did not notice. The soft wind began to build strength, pushing clouds along, hurrying them away from the estate, to pass across the moon and venture out over the night time lands. George was alone. He did not notice the estate's sigh, as the wind began to funnel down their various rounds, or the cloud's absent-minded wanderings. All this passed him by. In fact, all productive thought inside George's head came to a sudden halt. With a blank mind, George returned to his position on Richmond Road, where he had stood at 31 minutes past seven, staring forwards at the houses across from him. Waiting. Another light, a bit further down the road, went out. He stood still, hands hidden away in his pockets, as his feet enjoyed the firm, solid ground. At least that was real.

George began to think about another cigarette. His thoughts flocked to the idea of a cigarette. The flicker of his lighter's spark. The feeling of smoke. But all that ebbed away. Fell into obscurity upon George spotting a man, the same man he had seen moments before feverishly ranting to a vision of himself. The man hurried down Richmond Road. He seemed confused, out of place, or lost. He raced along the pavement, opposite to George, as a blue glow, a consistent glow, fell upon the man's rugged features. He wore a light grey tracksuit, a well-worn one, with patches of dirt clinging to the material in places. He caught sight of George, blankly staring across at him. A long, cold, silent stare passed between them. Passed the width of Richmond Road. George felt the cold again, creeping up on him. As the seconds grew longer, and the man flickered his attention between George and a certain spot on the pavement below the man's own trainers. George started to turn him over in his mind. The whole concept of him. How it was possible for him to be here, seemingly lost and cautious, but only minutes earlier standing and holding a figure of himself in a passionate manner. George felt like crying again. Nothing made sense. But his thoughts were torn apart, as the man sprang into the road and rushed towards him.

Fear crashed around him and George struggled to understand why. He backed away, as the man mounted the pavement and stepped towards him. Large steps. After one, George was in arm's length. After two, although George backed away, he was in the man's firm grasp. Holding George by the shoulders, the man took in his features. Scanning every detail. Exploring his face with blood shot eyes. George squashed the idea to flinch away, but felt that frightful urge creeping up his spine towards his head. He could smell the tracksuit. "How long you been here? Standing here?" The man asked, in a surprisingly measured tone.

"Not long," George stuttered.

"How long? I need...details."

"No more than...fifteen minutes."

"Fifteen minutes," he said, almost to himself, whispering the words. He relaxed his grasp on George and looked over his shoulder. For close to a minute, the bloodshot eyed man watched the blue light looming over the houses. George, following his gaze, noticed how the once flickering array now held a constant tone. He wanted to think it over, ponder upon it over a cigarette, but he was fully aware of the man's hand's, now resting around his arm.

The man's attention snapped back to George, as he frantically said, "You must stay here...right here."

"What? This spot?" George replied, momentarily finding the tone of his companion amusing.

"No, not exactly here, but Richmond. You must stay on Richmond Road."

"But why?" George stared deep into the red stained, blue eyes locked upon him. He saw a level of intelligence, overcome with some extreme emotion.

"   Cos..." The man trailed off, as something down Richmond Road caught his attention. "'Cos of that!" He barked, tightening his grip on George's shoulders and turning him to look in the direction he pointed. There stood George, in a state of confused horror. George, the one down the road from the one locked in the man's grasp, backed away, catching his leg on the car just behind him. There he fell and phased out of existence, like a dial had been turned and caused the features to dim and become transparent. George remembered falling. George remembered seeing himself with his present companion. George felt like crying. He heard the man say something, as he loosed his grip and disappeared into the surrounding shadows of the still night, but George did not catch it. He gazed down at the pavement, at the small section of ground before him and let the cold air gather about his shoulders.

It could have been hours that George stood, unmoving and lost in thought, until Josh pulled up alongside. The low rumble of his car broke the silence lingering in the air, rousing George form his current state. Slowly he clambered in. As Josh set the car on its way down Richmond Road, George sat in silence. Josh said a few words that landed on deaf ears. George's mind was preoccupied. Trying and failing to reason with the unreasonable. Every time he attempted to define the events of the last couple minutes, the back of his mind confronted the rest and forced a distant memory, from George's childhood, to resurface. He went to school round the corner from Richmond Road. His parents lived on the estate, just over the other side. Josh turned off Richmond and made for the main road, which led away from the estate. It was barely a minute later that it all collapsed.

There was a loud pop and the car lifted up a few centimetres. Josh swore and swerved for the curb. George grabbed his coat, sitting loosely around him, lacking anything else to hold on to. The familiar shape of the packet of cigarettes, deep within his pockets, reached out to him. Calling from below the layers of fabric, "Relax, all's well that ends well." Josh clambered out, staring back the way they came with a deep horror gripping his body. He froze, looking back at the estate. George slowly climbed out of the car, after a moment of staring blankly through the windscreen. Dust began to settle there, a growing layer, so that it started to be difficult to look out. George straightened up to stand on the pavement in the cold night air. A wave of calm swept him, to his own surprise, as he looked upon a crater. The blue light had gone, stifled out. Destroyed. The closest houses around the pair had large gashes taken out, as a snowy ash began to fall about them. They hadn't noticed this yet. "What...happened?" muttered Josh, having stumbled back to slump himself in the driver's seat, feet hanging out into the road. He would not say another word for the following hour. George looked into the crater, worked out where Richmond Road would have been and smiled. An unhappy smile. One caused by a sinking, almost drowning sensation that had taken hold of him. The centre of the crater would have been the house George stared across at, where the blue lights flickered from. Forming an inconsistent glow. Out of the entire road, the back rooms of three semi-detached houses still stood. Like cardboard cut outs.

The Creature

It could have been a creature. I'm not too sure. The thing grew and shrunk, moulding itself into different shapes. At one time it was a slimy eel, which slivered along the grimy floor, inspecting small cracks and unusual changes in elevation between floor boards. Another moment, the creature was a black mass of hovering smoke. It took this form for an extended period of time, usually between animals. The dense, shadowy fog floated a couple inches above the floor, changing the proportions of its shape, but never its form.

Of course it took the form of animals, like the aforementioned eel, but only very occasionally. I watch it do this, cigarette in hand, transfixed. I didn't move when it came closer, or follow when it disappeared round the side of a bag. A cycle of hovering as the black mass, to roaming the filthy room as some strange animal, before returning to that black, shapeless form. It began to regularly take its black mass form before the door and, in the shape of an animal, just sit in the same spot, peering across the room at me.

After the cycle had repeated a few times, and as I took a long breath of smoke, the creature took the form of a gentle looking black and white dog. The dog's eyes were the brightest blue I'd ever seen, shining out from deep within endless, hollow caverns. It just sat, watching me slowly exhale. As I looked on, through a hazy cloud of smoke, the dog's features began to melt and fall away. The dog's flesh piled up before it, pulsating in rhythm to my own runaway heart. I put the cigarette to my lips. Don't panic, I thought. It will all go away if I just don't panic. The flesh became a brighter, crimson red, burning my retinas. A permanent imprint of that dog's flesh, mingled with the now changing creature.

The crimson died away, becoming a darker version of the same colour, until it was an endless black. Strange and unnatural movements vibrated through the pulsating pile of flesh. But it was that form no longer. It was the eel, once again, slivering round and round the floor, following its tail. Round and round it went. I held the cigarette to my lips one final time, before putting it out. Abandoned by the cigarette, I watched the eel alone. After hundreds of laps, the eel slivered around the side of the door.

I didn't dare follow it. All my mind would allow me to do was stare, as if the spot where that pile of flesh had been would give some answers. No answers came. Possibly, because no questions were asked. Snatching up my coat, I timidly opened the door. No dog. No eel. No black mass. Slamming the door, I ran from the house. I ran until my breath escaped me, but still that crimson red was in front of me. Stained upon my retinas.

The experience of Philip Waterfield

Dear Mr Cambell,

I must by pass all formalities and move onto the main reason that I am writing to you. My Lord, dear friend, how my heart has raced these last few days. The mind haunts me with visions of what I have seen, so that I can't bear it anymore. I simple must inform someone of what my feeble eyes have been witness to. Jim, the following pages may lead you down a path of thinking, but I beg you to trust that, as I write this, I am of sound mind. At least as sound of mind as I could possibly be. Just trust in me that all included within these pages did really happen and isn't some fabrication of my mind. I thank you in advance.

So, I believe it to be the 13th of November, I left the house to venture out on a walk. I'd fancied taking my mind off the work, as the fresh air would do my caged mind some good. Under the impression that my paintings would profit off my exploration of the woods just overlooking the house, of which I had been taking attempts at painting, I set off towards the tree line. I followed the snaking road as best I could, as snow had taken over the country side the night prior. It came apparent, as I struggled through the deep winter coating, that there were no other tracks in the snow. By then it had just become the later part of the afternoon, and I was certain, despite the inconveniences of the weather, that old Farmer Lee would move down my way upon his root to market. I was certain of this, Jim. Not only had he done it before, as two years ago he got stuck just before my cottage where I had to help him free, but I distinctly remember hearing low, brutally clear rumbling coming from the road. It was so clear Jim that I could hear it on the opposite side of the house, from where I was painting. The undisturbed snow didn't strike me as unusual at the time, but in the days that followed that seemingly minor trick of the brain haunted me. It crept into my dreams. The very failure of my subconscious. Towering visions of bulky creatures, treading across the countryside without disturbing a single inch of snow floated through me. What ungodly creatures they must have been!

I'm sorry Jim; I became distracted and meandered from my narrative. I must try and stay to the events in as accurate a continuity as possible. I followed the lane up into the wood, taking the right path at the fork in the road towards the top of the hill, which led me into the frozen halls of wood. Oh God! Leaving the gloomy, grey clouds behind, hidden under layers of floundering branches, which sends shivers down my spine just remembering the subtle crunch of each step, leading me away. I don't believe my nerves can take much more of this, Jim. I will try to keep this as straight forward as possible. Please believe that I tried.

There was something in the very air of that wood that seemed unnatural. A rebellion against God. Mother Nature was everywhere. I looked, but some strong current in the air, that I breathed, seemed to push her away. The Grand Mother of the trees and supporter of the lush life, present in the spring months, would not welcome me. Her kin surrounded me, but she had not been there to nurture them. It simple couldn't be that Mother Nature had abandoned this wood, dense with once green life. I could feel the skin crawling current that replaced the air of nature. I continued on my walk, regarding how the once peaceful nature had drained. Finding myself looking at every inch of my surroundings, almost memorising them, I stopped dead in my tracks when, upon the path ahead of me, a man suddenly appeared where there was no man before. In fact, the snow around him was unbroken. No tracks of where he had come from, Just seas of white snow.

I stopped dead, at a distance from him, terrified of his nature. My train of thought began to deviate from certainty I had at the complete absences of a man ahead of me before hand, choosing to linger on doubt. In my momentary frozen state, a jolt of panic shuck my bones, as I recognised the worn jacket, jet black scarf and squashed cap. For they were my own. I swear on it Jim. They were, in fact, the articles of clothing I was wearing that very day. I even looked down at the scarf and jacket secured on my person, to be certain of the fact. It became impossible for me to move, or even call out, but while I stared across at him, the man turned. Turned and looked me dead in the eye. I recognised that face too. That was my own, the one I see each time I glance into a mirror, twisted into confusion and pure terror. I felt the muscles in my face twitch to match his expression. Oh Jim, how I wished to die. I couldn't bear it. The entire wood seemed to come crashing about me, as I stood transfixed on the spitting image of myself. I couldn't force my brain to understand it. Myself standing before me. A mere six yards, or so. It was as if the surrounding trees folded over each other, moulding into a black void. Only leaving the crystal ground.

There was only him and I. Or Just I. Us and that abyss of snow. A sensation of falling swept my body, but the secure snow wrapped around my shoes, encapsulating them. I struggled in finding any meaning in the occurring events, as I floated away from myself. It was only me then. Left to fall away from the wood. A rising sensation began to stir at the bottom of my throat, as my mind turned inside attempts to explain both the feeling of plummeting through gust of air, which surrounded my body and the firm pressure around my shoes as well. I looked down to check that snow held to my feet. . The pressure was not from snow, but sand. Thick, ash coloured sand. The seas of white snow had now been polluted by grey.

The falling sensation violently dissipated, but my head continued to rock back and forth. Slowly, raising my head to the sky, a deep orange glow passed over me. Where the wood had been, no more than seconds before, sat grand expanses of grey dunes. Rising and falling before me, all the way to the horizon. And what hung in the sky. Oh, Jim! Rising above the horizon, at a steady pace, a planet hung, shining that deep orange glow across me. It couldn't have been. But there it was. In the sky above me, as clear as the ink on this page. I could see it all so clearly, like looking through a telescope, as it rested so close.

The planet flew across the sky, towering over me seemingly seconds after I'd first seen it creep out from below the horizon. From the surface, a dense pack of blue structures, almost buildings, shone out towards me. As the planet rotated in its orbit, the expanse of blue mass appeared to move across the barren expanse of orange landscape. What a mighty city it must have been. Deserted in that orange wasteland. Even from my distance, I could almost make out architecture of the most heavenly beauty. The brightest blue I'd ever seen. A city of Gods. Oh, Jim! What a wondrous city! As I watched that metropolises cross the sky above me, a shape caught my eye. Just as the city began to move towards the dark side of the planet, a monstrous shape erupted from the ground. I couldn't contain myself, and forgive me for my handwriting, as I watched that figure claw its way free of the planet's surface. Free to stand to its full, imposing stature. Jim, the size of that thing. It could cover half of the colossal expanse of the city in only one step. I squirmed as it moved closer to that blue heaven. The shape, with its lanky limbs and giant head, hands and feet, raced towards the city. I couldn't take it, so shut my eyes as tight as I could. Falling to my knees I held the grey sand in my fists.

How could that monster move towards that heaven of beauty with such a destructive step? How could that planet even hang above me as it did? It was all too much, Jim. Please forgive me, for this is all too much. Please, Jim, forgive me. I stood up, tearing my eyes open to face the landscape once more. I let the sand fall from my hand.

Before me was the snowy wood. The harsh white snow almost blinded me. There was no planet in the sky. Just grey clouds. As quickly as the experience tore my senses apart in its arrival, it simply disappeared. I stood, in complete shock for a couple seconds, before the sensation of being watched rushed over me. Forgetting myself, I spun round and was forced into eye contact with myself. I struggled to control my breathing, as the man before me, myself, began to display a face of pure terror. I hardly had a second to take in the event unfolding before me, as I vanished. Without the blinking, I just vanished. One second I was standing there before me, then the next nothing. Just a disturbed patch of snow. No noise. No Movement. Nothing. Just gone.

I could have collapsed right then and there, but I gathered the energy from somewhere to run home. My legs wouldn't stop. With all my energy, I leaped through the snow, convinced that I was being pursed. Racing through the front door, it was locked in the following second and I'd locked myself away in my study. From there I watched the night fall over the wood, fearful of what lay within. Sleep evaded me that night and each night since. Horrifying visions of that creature marching forth from the wood came to me each time my eyes were closed.

That all happened three days ago. I swear to it, upon my mother's grave, that what I just recounted did really happen. I beg you to believe me. I've thought about it every second of each day that has passed, but I am hopeless for an explanation for a cause of that or even its meaning. Please Jim, don't think me mad. Forgive me Lord, for anything I may have done to warrant such a bold reminder of your mighty power. I beg you, Jim! Help me!

Philip Waterfield